GRIZZLY TALES

'CAUTIONARY TALES FOR LOVERS OF SQUEAM'

NASTY LITTLE BEASTS

JAMIE RIX

Illustrated by Steven Pattison

WARNING
THIS BOOK IS STILL DANGEROUS
CLOSE THE COVER

Orion
Children's Books

DO NOT OPEN THE DOOR!
(F YOU ENTER)
THE DARKNESS
THERE IS NO GOING BACK

To Helen

First published in Great Britain in 2007
by Orion Children's Books
a division of the Orion Publishing Group Ltd
Orion House
5 Upper St Martin's Lane
London WC2H 9EA

A catalogue record for this book is available from the British Library.

Printed in Great Britain

ISBN 978 1 84255 549 1

NOW THAT YOU HAVE STUPIDLY OPENED THE DOOR, YOU MUST READ THESE SAFETY TIPS BEFORE PROCEEDING . . .

READING SAFETY TIPS

1. Read fast.

2. Do not stop for warm milk and cookies.

3. Do not listen to a word He says.

4. Do not look behind you.

5. Do not laugh at the wicked children or you will be given your own room.

6. Do not cry out, 'I've done that!' when the children behave badly or you will be given your own room.

7. If you are given your own room do not take it. Once locked inside He will never let you out.

8. Do not accept sweets from strangers or your teeth will rot.

9. Remember, remember The Fifth of November *(Sorry. Don't know how that got in here. Ed.)*

Good luck. You'll need it.

WELCOME TO

THE HOTHELL DARKNESS

BREAKFAST 7.30AM 9.30AM.
NO PETS UNLESS BY PRIOR
ARRANGEMENT WITH THE MANAGEMENT.
WE GUARANTEE YOU SERVICE
WITH ACUTE STABBING PAINS!

The Night-night Porter

Hello. You came. I've had my eye on you ever since you picked up the book. Luckily I've got my eyeballs in today. Some mornings I am in such a hurry to get to work that I forget to put them in. On such days I rely on my nose. It can smell a BAD CHILD at a thousand paces. You're a bit niffy, but I like that in a guest.

Were you worried that I wouldn't have any vacancies? Don't be. There are always vacancies at The Hothell Darkness. I keep a room for every child in the world. Your name is already on the door.

You'll like your room. I designed it myself. It has fresh crocodile-skin sheets, a mini-bat, scare-conditioning and hot and cold running cockroaches. Very shriek-chic.

You may not know who I am, but I know who you are. I even know where you USED to live. Would you mind if I asked you a few questions? Nothing too hard. I just want to check that you are beastly enough for The Darkness!

ANSWER TRUTHFULLY!

1) Have you ever told a lie? *Answer yes, because 'no' will be a lie.*

2) Have you ever laughed at an animal caged at the zoo? *They deserve it, don't they?*

3) Have you ever left food on the side of your plate? *I know I have!*

4) Have you ever slept the wrong way up in your bed? *Naughty, naughty!*

5) Have you ever stayed in a hothell before? *It doesn't matter. You're here now, that's all that counts. Please leave you parents' credit card at the desk.*

Well done! You are BAD and have failed with flying colours! You win an indefinite stay with me in The Darkness for ever.

I just know that you and I are going to have such fun together! Now that you are down here for ever, you must acquaint yourself with your fellow guests/prisoners/torture victims.* To help you get started I have selected a few of their

* delete where applicable

personal stories from our Visitor's Book, or as I prefer to call it The Book of Grizzly Tales. These are their tales as told to me.

Boo hoo! Boo hoo!

Oink! Oink!

Gurgle! Goo-goo!

I wan—I wan—I wan—I w—

Heeeeeeeeeeeeeeeeeeeeeeeeelp!

Squeak! Squeak! Splat!

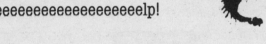

SHUT UP! HOW MANY TIMES DO I HAVE TO TELL YOU?

Honestly, those guests! Noisy bunch of ingrates. It's not enough that I feed them and change their water every week, they want to be let out as well! What do they think this is, an hotel?

Well, it is, of course. I know it's called a *hothell*, but really that's just an hotel with fiery pits.

And very happy YOU'RE going to be here, too.

Now, the children in these tales live in the ANIMAL WING of the hothell, not because their evil minds are UN-STABLE, but because they all have one thing in common: they are all NASTY LITTLE BEASTS!

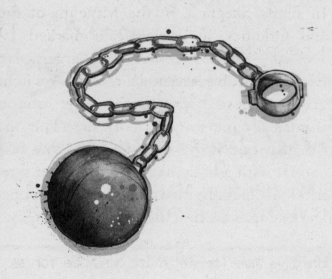

THE GRUB A-BLUB-BLUB

In sunny Skegness, in the Museum of Freaks and Oddities, in a glass case marked DO NOT FEED, lives the largest, laziest witchetty grub ever known to man. A witchetty grub, for those of you who've never eaten one, is normally the size of a corn dog. The one in the glass case is the size of a corn cow. It's big and fat with a body like stacked rubber tyres. It lives on a diet of pizzas, milkshakes and popcorn and occupies its time by watching the telly.

> Oh. I do love The Telly. It's to blame for so much bad behaviour!

The museum has nicknamed it the Grub A-Blub-Blub, because at night time it cries itself to sleep. Not surprising really, because it's not a grub at all!

✳ ✳ ✳

Savannah Slumberson was cursed. Not by trolls or bad fairies, but by her parents. They belonged to that select breed of adult who believes that life is best lived outdoors. Never a weekend passed when they weren't out scaling peaks or yomping through bogland or cycling the Pennine Way. They liked being cold and wet. They preferred their clothes sticky and damp. They looked forward to blisters and welcomed a wind-burn or three. If you asked Savannah's parents to choose between a weekend break in a posh hotel, or sleeping with badgers and digging a hole for a loo, they were hole diggers every time! Their hallway was a monument to the Great Outdoors, piled high with walking sticks, muddy boots and steaming woollen socks with that unmistakable tang of unwashed yak.

Savannah was cursed because her parents were ramblers and *she*, most definitely, was not. The furthest Savannah liked rambling was from the warmth of her bed to the fridge. The closest she liked being to the weather was watching it on the telly or thumbing her nose at it through the window. Savannah was a lie-a-bed, a slovenly sloth, who despised everything her parents stood for and made it her daily task to do the exact opposite of whatever they wanted her to do.

Mornings in the Slumberson house always followed a similar pattern. Savannah would lie in while her parents rose with the lark and made preparations for that day's excursion. Then, at seven o'clock sharp, they would wake Savannah up by flinging back the curtains and opening the window. It was always a source of acute embarrassment when her parents tramped into her bedroom, coiled with ropes and crampons, wearing khaki shorts and hard hats!

'With a step and a stamp
And a heave and a ho,
It's a mighty hearty tramp
And a Ramb-er-ling we go!'

As they sang out of tune, Savannah pulled the duvet up around her ears.

'Oh come on, Savvy, sweetie!' pleaded her mother. 'You'll love it at the summit.'

'Summit!' yelled Savannah. 'What summit?'

'It's only a *little* mountain,' said her father.

'Do I look like a goat?' growled Savannah. 'Because you must be confusing me with something that LIKES it up mountains! Go away. You're depressing me!'

But Savannah's parents never went away. They just kept coming on like a bad dose of stomach cramps. If she locked her bedroom door and tried to stay in bed all day, they would attach grappling hooks to her window sill and climb up ropes to reach her. Then they'd knock on her window and whisper quietly through the glass.

'Oh, Savannah! Oh, Savannah, darling! It's time to get up!'

Which was why Savannah spent her whole life being never less than grumpy.

But thankfully that was all about to change! For the worse!

Boo hoo! Boo hoo!

16

> Oh, do shut up and have another twelve pizzas!

* * *

Back in March when the Slumberson family were choosing a summer holiday, Savannah had begged her parents to take her to a bed and breakfast in Bridlington where, for two whole weeks, she could indulge her twin passions for bed and breakfast. But her parents had a special treat for her instead.

'We're going on a camping holiday!' trilled her mother one morning. 'In a tent with sleeping bags.'

Her father's eyes were gleaming with excitement. 'It's going to be such fun. Cooking on an open fire, early-rising, cycling to—'

'*Cycling!*' Savannah was lying wrapped in her duvet on the sofa scoffing waffles when her father unleashed this latest surprise. The shock shot an unchewed lump of waffle down her windpipe and made her choke.

'Yes, cycling,' said her father. 'We're taking the bikes! Why else would I have bought you these?' And he produced a plastic bag from behind his back. If there was one thing Savannah loathed more than cycling it was cycling lycra! Body-hugging, dog sick-coloured clothes that showed off every lump and body-bump.

'I am not wearing those!' she yelled. 'You will have to put me under general anaesthetic before I let you near me with a stitch of that!'

But parents being parents, with greater powers than even the police, they confiscated her television and said that they would recycle it in the river if she didn't do as she was told.

'I hate you,' seethed Savannah when she gave in. 'I'm only doing this because you're blackmailing me. Just because I'm coming with you this year does not mean that I shall ever be going on holiday with you again!'

A truer truth wath never spake!

* * *

 By seven o'clock the following morning, Mr and Mrs Slumberson were ready on the front lawn, standing astride their bicycles, which were

18

laden with rucksacks, cooking equipment, hurricane lamps, bedding rolls and a family tent. It was a six-hour ride to the campsite so they were keen to get going. Savannah had been dragged reluctantly out of bed, and had tried every trick in the book to be left behind: sitting on the loo for two hours, pretending to forget her luggage fourteen times and suddenly feeling ill.

'I think it might be rickets,' she whimpered. 'Why don't you go on and I'll catch up when I'm better!' But her parents were having none of it.

'You're coming now!' shouted her father.

'It's not fair,' squawked his awkward daughter. 'I'm not even awake yet.'

'That's OK,' said her mother. 'The cycling will wake you up.'

'But ... But ...'

'What?'

Savannah wanted to say that the lycra made her look like a walrus and she wasn't coming, but she knew what her parents would say.

'Where we're going, Savannah, it doesn't matter what you look like. Sheep have no interest at all in how you look.'

This is untrue. of course. Some sheep are very snappy dressers. Others look like mutton dressed as lamb. 'Baa ha ha!' is the sound of a sheep laughing at lycra.

✳ ✱ ✸

So off they went, but not before Savannah had pleaded cramp at the end of the road.

'Ow, it hurts!' she cried. 'Why does this always happen to me?'

'Take a rest and see how it is in a moment,' her father said stupidly.

'Jolly good,' said Savannah, wrapping herself up in her quilted sleeping bag and lying lengthways across her saddle and handlebars to get some long overdue shut-eye.

Savannah had got her way. Not only did she not have to cycle, but if she kept her eyes closed for the whole journey she would not have to see the appalled faces of passers-by when they heard her parents' embarrassing singing.

'Oh we're off on holiday,
Feeling full of beans, let's play.
Let's raise a cheer

'Cause we're nearly there.
Hip, hip, hip, hip hooray!'

This was how they arrived at the camping site, not six but *twelve* hours later – Mr and Mrs Slumberson puffing up front with their lazy 'Gosh!-Have-I-really-slept-through-the-whole-journey!' daughter in tow. It was with a certain amount of horror, however, that Savannah opened her eyes for a quick peek at her surroundings and saw a sign pinned to a tree by the side of the track that led into the forest:

FIT CAMP

She didn't like the sound of that!

The campsite owner, Mrs Evadne Sprite (a bony woman of advancing wrinkles who liked to keep active) was juggling with three medicine balls outside her lodge. The Slumbersons introduced themselves.

'Welcome to Fit Camp,' Mrs Sprite said. 'Turkish wrestling for the over-eighties at five o'clock tomorrow morning. Anyone interested? Savannah?'

'Can human beings get up at five o'clock?' yawned Savannah. 'Doesn't it kill them?'

'No more than staying in bed,' chuckled the old lady. 'So I'll put your name down, shall I?'

'Certainly not,' said Savannah. 'I'm not over eighty.'

'And never will be by the looks of things.' It was a mysterious thing for the old lady to say and was met by a cold stare from Savannah. 'Camp rules are as follows. Everyone to have a good time and nobody to stay in bed beyond sun-up!'

'What sort of a holiday's *that*?'

'A healthy sort of holiday,' said Mrs Sprite.

'Ugh!' Savannah pulled her sleeping bag tightly around her shoulders.

'Seize the day, before the day seizes you!' snarled Mrs Sprite in a tone that sounded less like a friendly word of advice and more like a mortal threat.

Suddenly, a disgustingly fat larva, the size of a large lump of snot, fell out of the sky and landed on top of Savannah's head. She screamed as it wriggled on her scalp and tangled itself up in her hair. She slammed her cycling helmet back onto her head and felt the bug burst. Its innards dripped down behind her ears like warm lemon curd. She looked up and screamed again. There were thousands of them hanging off the branches of the trees like giant-sized jelly babies.

'What are those?!' she cried.

'Witchetty grubs.' The old lady smiled a toothless grin. 'Lazy little beggars. In this neck of the woods, if you stand still for too long they'll hitch a ride on you. That's why I keep my campers moving. One-two! One-two! There's less chance of being witchettied!'

Savannah did not like this place.

'Get our tent up!' she bawled.

Heeeeeeeeeeelp

That's Monty.
Ignore him. It's
just a cry for
help.

Sensing a nightmare holiday in the making, Savannah decided that the best way to avoid the grubs and Mrs Sprite's exercise regime was to stay in bed and sleep for seven days. Her parents, 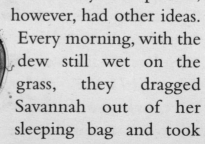 however, had other ideas. Every morning, with the dew still wet on the grass, they dragged Savannah out of her sleeping bag and took her on a trip to some place of local disinterest.

They took her to an old church, and stood in the cemetery in the pouring rain admiring the slate roof and thick stone walls.

'It's amazing to think,' said her father, 'that this is an old Norman church.'

Savannah licked the rain off the end of her nose. 'It might be amazing to Old Norman,' she grumbled, 'but it's as boring as billiards to me. I want to go back to bed.'

They visited a Roman aqueduct and stood underneath its towering arches.

'I could stand here and look at this all day!' beamed her mother.

'Then you must be dead!' sulked Savannah, leaning her head against the aqueduct and closing her eyes. 'You're only allowed to wake me up if it moves.'

And they visited the only lawnmower museum in the world.

'Fascinating things . . . lawnmowers,' said her father, lifting his head from the museum guide.

'Absolutely,' said Mrs Slumberson. 'Is that a *Qualcast 35S* I see?'

'Of course you do know why this is the only lawnmower museum in the world, don't you?'

interrupted Savannah, as she struggled to keep her eyelids open.

'No,' said her father. 'Why?'

'Because lawnmowers are so blinking BORING nobody other than you two wants to look at them!'

But when Savannah's parents announced a trip to Shinwell's oldest Sewage Works, Savannah put her foot down.

'I am having a lie-in,' she snarled turning over in her sleeping bag, 'and there's nothing you can do to stop me!' And with that she disobeyed not only her parents, but also the rules of Fit Camp!

✹ ✹ ✹

Over by the office, underneath a canopy of trees, Mrs Evadne Sprite was eating her breakfast: a big bowl of live witchetty grubs. She picked up each grub by its head and bit off the back end from just below its neck. Then she threw away the head while it was still twitching. The shock of hearing Savannah shout '*I'm having a lie in!*' made her bite down too hard and she accidentally swallowed a grub whole.

> A witchetty grub's head is full of poison and Mrs Sprite was immediately sick. The pain in her stomach, however, was but a gnat's wince compared to the pain that now awaited Savannah!

That night, after Savannah had spent the entire day in her sleeping bag eating pizzas, Mrs Sprite came to the Slumberson tent and offered to take the girl's parents on a midnight bat walk.

SQUEAK! SQUEAK! SPLAT!

> You're not going anywhere, Cherie.

'You'll be away all night,' Mrs Sprite told them, when they jumped at the chance.

'Savannah,' said Mrs Slumberson, 'do you mind if we leave you on your own tonight?'

'Whatever,' said the lazy girl. 'I'm not bothered.'

'The sleep will do her good,' the old lady said sarcastically. 'Only make sure you stay inside your tent,' she warned her. 'When there is a full moon the witchetty grubs are restless.'

Savannah snorted with derision. 'If you think I'll be leaving my sleeping bag out of choice,' she said, 'you must be crackers.'

'But I'm *not* crackers,' cackled Mrs Evadne Sprite, which rather implied that Savannah would be leaving her sleeping bag whether she liked it or not.

Six hours later, still on her own, and with a full moon hanging high in the sky, Savannah was woken by a strange plopping noise outside. It sounded like heavy drops of rain exploding on a lily pond. She switched on her torch and flicked the beam across the sides of the tent, but could see nothing. More plops. She flashed the torch upwards and was horrified to see that the canvas roof of the tent was heaving. It had sagged in the middle and was nearly touching her head. She had to get out before it split and showered her with whatever foul things were up there!

Frantically gathering her sleeping bag around her for protection, she unzipped the front flaps of the tent and slithered out into the forest to see what was causing the bulge. Her blood froze. It was raining witchetty grubs! They dripped off the trees like thick slime and bounced off the tent's roof, using it like a trampoline to flip down the back of Savannah's neck and into her sleeping bag!

She did all she could to swat them off her skin. She screamed and threw herself back inside the tent. She tried to zip the flaps up to stop this invasion of sluggery, but thousands of grubs slithered through the opening and overwhelmed her. They cocooned her where she lay, binding her into her sleeping bag with a sticky gossamer web that closed her eyes and stopped her from screaming.

Then, with their work complete and the sun nearly up, they slithered slowly back to bed on the overhanging branches of the trees.

It's a bit too late to blub now!

Boo hoo! Boo hoo!

When Mr and Mrs Slumberson returned a few minutes later, their daughter was nowhere to be seen. They found a large, lazy witchetty grub inside the tent, which Mr Slumberson chucked out while Mrs Slumberson waved her arms and shrieked.

Then they left the camp site for good, vacating their lot for an outdoor family from sunny Skegness. It just so happened that the husband was the curator of a Museum for Freaks and Oddities!

And Mrs Evadne Sprite? She still takes her breakfast in the open air, under the canopy of trees. This morning she was singing a new song.

'Stitchetty twitchetty
Witchetty grub
Fat as a corn cow
And lacking in love.
Stitchetty twitchetty
Witchetty grub
In bed now for ever
So why do you blub?'

I've just had great news! The Museum for Freaks and Oddities is closing next year, because the cost of Savannah's pizzas has bankrupted them. When it finally shuts she's coming here. I've prepared Room 492.567 for her. I've called it The Kebab Suite. She can still watch telly all day, but she has to stand up to do it. It's not as cruel as it sounds. She doesn't have to support her own weight, because I'll be replacing her backbone with a high-tensile metal skewer. She'll never get bored, because I'll be constantly changing her view by turning her in never-ending circles. And she'll never get cold, because I'll be heating the room to 100 degrees centigrade with a stainless steel electric grill. The only thing I won't be doing is pizzas, not in The Kebab Suite. If she's hungry, I'll just give her some pitta bread and a bacon slicer and she can carve a bit of flesh off her own body!

The room next to Savannah's belongs to a devilish boy called Monty.

31

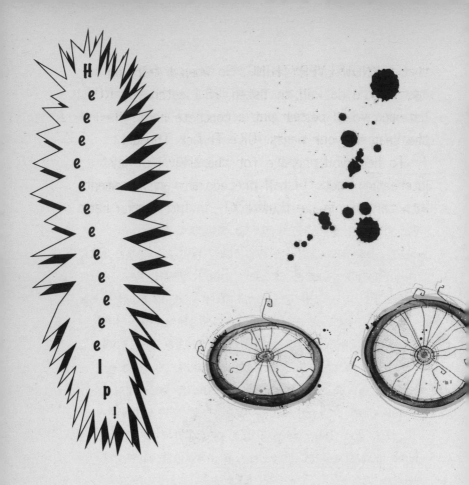

Heeeeeeeeelp!

At least, the room would belong to Monty if Monty lived there. I've given him permission to live off the premises with a group of wicked children called The Sewer Rats. I'm not going soft. The place they live in is so vile and disgusting that there isn't a room in this hothell that can better it!

Now, all the children down here will tell you

that I KNOW EVERYTHING. So when I tell you facts you'd do well to listen. If I catch you NOT listening you'd better put a concrete roof tile in the seat of your pants. OK? Thwack Thwack!

To help you prepare for the arrival of my interesting facts I shall precede any announcement with this simple heading: NEXT—An Interesting Fact.

When you see NEXT—An Interesting Fact you
should brace yourself for a dose of learning. I
know you get enough learning at school. I know it
makes you cross and badly behaved . . . and that's
rather what I'm hoping for!

NEXT—AN INTERESTING FACT

On planet Earth 27,000 animal species
become extinct every year. That's seventy-four
per day, or to put it another way, ten species
on each of the seven continents, which means
that in Great Britain alone there is one
species popping its clogs every week. I know
which species died out this week. It's the little
known Really Horrid Brother Called Monty Who
Thinks It's Acceptable To Bully His Sister And
Make Her Scream And Scream By Teasing Her
With Exotic Pets Like Creepy Crawlies And
Snakes species, which can generally be found
at Brown Trouser Farm, Piddlepants on the
Wold, Cheshire.

MONTY'S PYTHON

Monty was a bad boy. He was a home-based terrorist, who lurked in the shadows of the farmhouse where he lived, stalking his soppy little sister, Mayflower: chasing her, pinning her down and threatening her with all sorts of WOMD, otherwise known as Wrigglies of Mass Dread.

For example, if she was playing nicely in the buttercup meadow, building a fairy ring out of freesias and crocuses, Monty would sneak up behind her, and drop something sharp and hard down her back of her dress.

'Scorpion!' he'd cry.

To which Mayflower's response was predictably, '*AAAAAAAAAAGH!*'

Monty would then split his sides while his petrified sister, with eyes as big as porcelain door knobs, ran through their mother's flowerbed shredding her dress on the thorns. Only when Monty spotted his parents charging up the garden path did he hurriedly admit to his deception to shut his sister up. 'It's a carrot, you baby!'

When his parents weren't there, however, Monty's wicked teasing reigned supreme. His favourite time of day was bedtime. In the *dark*, a girl's imagination runs wild. Rarely did Mayflower go to bed without something cold and slimy brushing against her feet, and in the shadows a ghostly voice whispering in her ear. 'That's worms in your bed, that is!'

And Mayflower never gave anything less than a lung-bursting scream by way of reply.

'AAAAAAAAAAAAAAAGH!'

Only it was never worms in her bed. 'It's licorice!' sniggered Monty.

✳ ✳ ✳

Mayflower had lost count of the number of times Monty had sprung out from behind the fridge at breakfast and thrown something glistening into her cereal.

'Ugh!' he shouted. 'Mayflower's a freak! She likes slugs in her cornflakes.'

In fact, he'd done it once too often. So much so that even Mayflower, the wettest fish in the bucket, stopped screaming.

'I'm not an idiot, Monty,' she sneered. 'I know they're not slugs. What are they really?' It never crossed her mind that Monty might be double-bluffing.

'Slugs!' he cried gleefully.

'*AAAAAAAAAAAAAAAGH!*'

At which point Mayflower rushed from the room to be sick, leaving Monty chuckling to himself and pondering his evil genius!

'They're marshmallow chunks!' he snickered cruelly. 'You big girl!'

But just as Mayflower grew weary of these games, so too did Monty. After years of teasing his little sister with pretend bugs and slugs her screams began to bore him. He needed a louder, more terrified response to keep his interest alive, and where better to turn, he thought, than pets.

Mayflower loved her pets; the cuddlier the better. She gave them soppy names, and told them lovely stories, and when they died she buried them in lace-trimmed cardboard shoeboxes. But Monty was not thinking cuddly. Cuddly was for *girls*. The pet he had in mind was beastlier by design!

❋ ❋ ❋

He bought his pet python from a pet shop. He went in with an empty carrier bag and came out with it bulging. The pet shop owner – a man with porcupine eyebrows – had been most insistent that Monty bought some live mice as well.

'Why?' asked the boy. 'To keep the snake company?'

'No,' said the pet shop owner. 'For lunch.'

For one horrible moment, Monty thought that the pet shop owner meant lunch for him, but of course he didn't.

The first scream from Mayflower was twice as loud as any that Monty had ever extracted. She was in her bedroom making glitter galoshes with her pet parrot, Polly, when the snake appeared over her shoulder, announced its arrival with a long hiss in

38

her ear and tickled her cheek with its tongue.

'Oh my *AAAAAAAAAAGH!!*' she screamed, shaking the pictures off the wall. 'Take it away. What is it?'

Monty stepped round from behind her. 'It's my new pet python,' he smiled, 'called SisterEater.' The name did its job and brought forth a second scream, which bounced around the bedroom like a rubber bullet and exploded in the light bulb. 'Its jaws are so huge,' continued Monty, 'it could fit all of you inside.'

'A … a … all of me?' stammered Mayflower.

'Yes, all of you!' roared Monty. 'Even your big feet and sticky-out pigtails. It could woofle you up like a single pea and still have room for pudding!'

Mayflower's brain could barely imagine a mouth so large and terrifying. It didn't have to. Monty got the snake to dislocate its lower jaw and show her.

'*AAAAAAAAAAAAAAAGH!*'

'What are you screaming at now?' Monty said innocently. 'I did tell you it had a big mouth so it can't be that.'

'No,' panted Mayflower, whose breaths were coming short and fast, 'a slimy green mouse just ran out of its mouth!'

She was not wrong. One of the live mice that Monty had bought from the pet shop had just sprinted across the snake's tongue, hopped over its teeth and run towards the skirting board.

'Oh yes,' said Monty casually. 'That was probably escaping from the snake's stomach. Snakes eat mice, you know.'

'But it was *alive*,' squeaked Mayflower.

'Of course it was! Don't you know anything about snakes? They only like to eat things if they're wiggling!'

'Wiggling!' she gasped.

'Wiggling,' he smirked. 'And you're the biggest wiggler I know!'

'AAAAAAAAAAAAAAAAGH!

Monty was going to have endless hours of fun with his sister!

✳ ✳ ✳

He woke her the next morning with a breakfast tray.

'Wakey wakey!' he cried, drawing her bedroom curtains to let in the sun. 'I've brought you a mice cup of tea in bed!'

Mayflower yawned and rubbed her eyes. 'Thank you,' she said. 'Oh look, you've left the tea bag in the mug.' But when she grabbed the string to pull it out, it wasn't a string at all. It was a dead mouse's tail.

'AAAAAAAAAAAAAAAGH!'

'It was an accident,' Monty explained a few moments later, when his sister crept into the kitchen for a proper breakfast. 'I don't know what possessed that mouse to climb into your mug of tea. Maybe it was just thirsty.'

'Are you telling me the truth?' whispered Mayflower.

'Of course I am,' he replied. 'You're my sister. I love you.' And he was so convincing that she believed him. 'I really am sorry if I've upset you,' he continued. 'Will you let me make it up to you?'

'All right,' she smiled, feeling safe at last.

'Then sit down,' he said, tucking a napkin into the neck of her T-shirt. 'I've made you breakfast.'

'What is it?' she asked, as Monty placed an egg cup in front of her containing a round brown egg.

'It's a boiled mouse,' he said, flicking the lifeless tail and stiff little legs to make them wobble.

'AAAAAAAAAAAAAAAAGH!'

* * *

Later that evening, he pursued her into the bathroom, where it was Mayflower's habit to take a bath with the shower curtain drawn. This was perfect for Monty's purposes. He sneaked into the room undetected and with a cry of, 'Look out, there's a mouse in the house!' threw a live mouse over the top of the shower curtain. When it landed in Mayflower's bath water and started swimming, all hell broke loose.

'AAAAAAAAAAAAAAAGH!'

But Monty hadn't finished yet. While Mayflower flapped and yelled he pretended to come to her rescue. 'Never fear, SisterEater's here!' he proclaimed, sliding the snake into the water. 'He'll get rid of

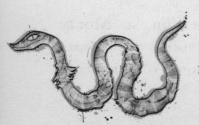

that mouse for you!'

You'd have thought a bomb had exploded!
While poor, screaming Mayflower dragged
 the curtain off its pole and flapped
around in the water like a petrified pig
in a crocodile pool, Monty left the
bathroom with a sly grin and a
casual quip over his shoulder.
'Have a mice day now!'

✻ ✻ ✻

After a week, however, things began to go
wrong for Monty. Because he was feeding his
python so many mice the snake had grown and
now that it was bigger, little mice no longer
satisfied its massive hunger. The python pinned
Monty up against his bedroom wall, while its
stomach grumbled like a drain, and demanded
something bigger.

'You don't mean me, do you?' said the boy
nervously. 'Because I *am* your master, and
traditionally pets are not allowed to eat their
masters.'

The snake did *not* mean him, so Monty
introduced the python to his sister's pet parrot.

'Polly, SisterEater. SisterEater, Polly,' he said,

opening Polly's cage so that the two pets could shake hands. Only SisterEater didn't have a hand to shake. When Mayflower trotted into the bedroom a few moments later, her precious parrot was nowhere to be seen. Actually, that's not quite true. She could see its shape bulging halfway down the snake's neck and hear its muffled voice, 'Who's a tasty boy, then?'

Needless to say, she screamed.

'AAAAAAAAAAAAAAAAGH!'

Unfortunately, Monty was now caught in a vicious circle. Eating the parrot had made the snake grow again, which meant that Monty now had to find something even larger to feed it on. His eyes settled on his sister's cat, snuggled warmly in front of the fire.

When Mayflower came skipping into the sitting room with a ball of wool in her hand and called out, 'Cuddles. Oh Cuddles. It's playtime, Cuddles!' she saw something she never thought she'd see. 'Why is SisterEater curled up in front of the fire?' she asked uneasily.

'He's tired,' smiled Monty. 'He's just eaten.'

'So where's my pussy cat, Cuddles?' she cried.

'You haven't—?'

'I have!' sniggered her brother, kicking SisterEater awake. The python sat up showing off the lump of cat in its throat.

'Miaow,' came the muffled voice of Cuddles.

'AAAAAAAAAAAAAAAAAGH!

came the clarion voice of Mayflower. Then she dropped the ball of wool and fled the room.

After the cat, it was Mayflower's pet lamb, Dimples. The python ambushed it while it was gambolling through the buttercup meadow and gobbled it up in one bite.

'AAAAAAAAAAAAAAAAAGH!

I'm going to treat you to one of my songs.
Baa baa, black sheep
Have you any head?
No, sir, no, sir
I think I'm dead.

After the lamb it was a small horse. Well, Mayflower's pony to be exact. Mayflower and her best friend, Miranda, had been riding it in the paddock when Miranda disappeared.

'Oh Monty!' cried Mayflower. 'Have *you* seen Miranda?'

'I don't think I have,' said Monty. 'No, wait a moment. What's that?' He pointed into the paddock where a large python, its stomach distended with the bulk of a pony and rider, was jumping a five-bar gate. 'Is that her in the saddle?'

'*AAAAAAAAAAAAAAAAGH!*

And after the pony? A cow. And after the cow? A coachload of tourists visiting the farm shop. And after the coach load of tourists visiting the farm shop? Well, nothing!

Mayflower had run out of pets and the farm had run out of big animals. There was nothing left to feed to Monty's python. Monty did consider sacrificing his sister, but his mother put a stop to that. She took one look at her daughter marinating in a pot with a giant python drooling over the top of her, and threw herself across the table as a human shield.

'*Don't you dare!*' she yelled at Monty.

'You're quite right,' he said, leading his python

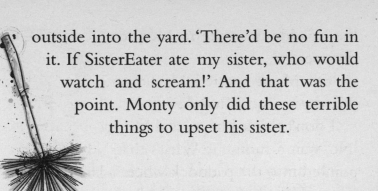

outside into the yard. 'There'd be no fun in it. If SisterEater ate my sister, who would watch and scream!' And that was the point. Monty only did these terrible things to upset his sister.

But it didn't work out quite as Monty planned!

H
E
E
E
E
E
E
E
E
L
P
!

With no food, Monty had come to the end of the line.

There was only one thing he could do with his pet.

'You can't throw it away!' shrieked Mayflower. 'I thought you didn't like it,' said Monty, who had the snake's head in one dustbin, its tail in another and the coils of its body in six more.

'I *don't* like it,' said Mayflower. 'I hate it. But you can't put a pet in the bin just because it's too big.'

'Then I shan't,' said Monty. 'I shall flush it down the loo instead!'

He was at it for days, pushing every coil around the bend with the loo brush. In the end, it was too big to flush away entirely and too heavy to pull back up and start again. This meant, of course, that Monty had to leave it down the pan and couldn't go to the loo.

'Are you scared of being bitten?' giggled Mayflower.

'No,' he said, when he *was*. 'Are you?'

'Not at all,' said his sister, who had miraculously come out of her shell since saving the python from the dustbin. 'In fact, because I saved his life, SisterEater and I are the best of friends now,' she said. 'He lets me go to the loo whenever I want. But you, on the other hand—' she burst into peals of laughter '—you'll just have to cross your legs for the rest of your whole life!'

'You're enjoying this, aren't you?' he said.

'Oh yes!' she cried. 'Because you'll *have* to go sometime, and when you do, SisterEater will burst out of the bowl and bite your winkle off! Ha ha ha!' And she didn't stop laughing all night.

I love this job. Take a timid girl like Mayflower. Not a bad bone in her body. The chances of her booking into The Darkness? Zero. Then one day she meets a python who brings out the brute in her and I'm rushed off my hooves getting her hothell room ready!

❋ ❋ ❋

On the fourth night of not using the loo, Mayflower's prediction came true. Monty could not keep his legs crossed any longer. Despite the obvious danger, he dashed into the smallest room in the house, where — as you might have guessed — the hacked-off demon of the deep was waiting to grab him. With a zip and a splash and an almighty chomp, Monty disappeared around the bend with his head in the jaws of a python!

When Monty came round, he could hear running water. The air was dank and fetid. A taste not unlike bad eggs clung to the back of his throat. He opened his eyes slowly to find that he was perched on a narrow ledge with his feet dangling in a stream of thick, brown, slow-moving water. He was in the sewers.

Looking either side, he was astonished to see thousands of glum-faced children sitting on the ledge next to him. Around their necks, each of them was wearing a collar which had a small metal name-tag attached. The tags jangled softly like cow bells and echoed eerily off the curved brick walls.

'What's the matter with you lot?' Monty said, pointing down the long Victorian tunnel which narrowed to a tiny dot of light at the end. 'Down there. Look! There's a way out.' Nobody seemed that pleased. Instead, a small girl with pale white skin and dark rings around her eyes tapped him on the shoulder.

'You're not going anywhere,' she said, pointing across the sludgy stream at the wall opposite.

Monty looked up and gasped. Thousands of sparkling eyes stared back at him through the darkness. The wall was lined with watching animals: crocodiles, spiders, praying mantises, hamsters, mice, snapping turtles, crabs, rats, snakes and scorpions.

'This is *our* place,' they hissed menacingly. 'You're *our* pets now!'

Monty felt around his own neck and jumped with fright. He too was wearing a collar. 'Are those all your pets?' he asked the other children. 'The pets that you got bored with and flushed down the loo?'

'Yes,' trembled the pale-faced girl. 'They keep us here for their amusement, and when they don't want us anymore, they eat us!'

'Right, I'm off!' roared Monty, and he plunged off the ledge into the river of stink. 'You can't keep me here!' he screamed, as he swam towards the light.

'Oh yesss I can!' boomed a voice from the shadows. Suddenly, SisterEater dropped down in front of Monty and opened wide his jaws. His mouth was as big as the tunnel itself. 'You can run if you like,' said Monty's python, 'but I'm soooo hungry, I might just bite! Go on, Monty. Make my day!'

But Monty thought he wouldn't. On balance, he felt, it was better to stay put and do as he was told, like an obedient little pet.

He's still down there now; still fetching sticks; still hoping his master won't get bored and eat him. If you don't believe me. do what Mayflower does every night before bed. She puts her head down the pan and listens for her brother's cries. And when she hears him call out.

'Heeeeeeeeeeeeeeeeelp!'

she laughs *Aagh-ha-ha-ha-ha-a,* a cold little laugh of revenge.

I must confess. it's very satisfying when bad children do my work for me. The Sewer Rats are already captives in a living hell. so that lets me out of having to house them here in The Darkness.

It saves me having to cough up for food and gives me more empty rooms for children like YOU! By the way when I say 'cough up for food', I do mean what I say. Never knock a phlegm sandwich till you've tried one!

Excuse me a moment

That should shut him up for a while!

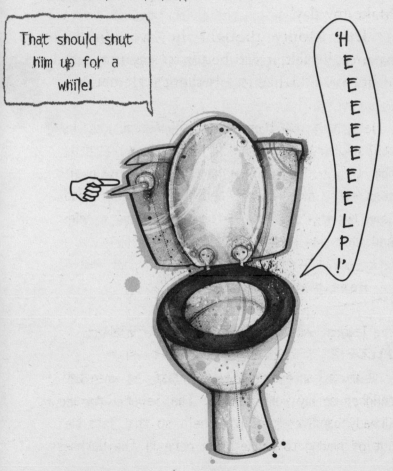

'HEEEEEEELP!'

53

'I wan—!'

Not now.

Talking of food, have you ever heard a lobster scream? Cry out in pain as it's PLUNGED into boiling water by a chef? If you have you're the only person in the world, because lobsters don't scream. They die the second they touch the water. Greedy little girls, on the other hand, are quite a different kettle of cuttle. They make a terrible noise when they're boiled, which is probably why you've never seen GIRL THERMIDOR on menus in top restaurants.

You do in restaurants down here, though!

I've got a greedy little girl in Room 492,561. Her name is Shannon Shellfish and she's greedier than every other greedy girl put together. She's quite pretty in a sort of stampy, pouty-faced way, but she makes herself look extremely unattractive by tagging the words 'I want' onto the front of every sentence.

'I wan—!'   Nothing! Give it a rest!

What she wants to say is, 'I want to get out of here right now!' but I don't want her to. And down here, what I want goes!

54

THE LOBSTER'S SCREAM

It started when Shannon Shellfish was very young. In the maternity hospital, thirty seconds after she was born, she took one look at her exhausted, weeping, puffy-eyed mother and shouted, **'I want a more beautiful mummy!'**

Two days later, when her parents took her home and she stared up at the house from inside her pram, she yelled, **'I want a bigger house!'** And on her first birthday she threw all of her presents back at her parents with a cry of, **'I want a week in EuroDisney!'**

As you can probably guess, Shannon's mother did not swap herself for a less tired mummy and her father did not sell the house, but they *did* take all her presents back to the shops and pay for a week at EuroDisney instead.

It didn't matter to Shannon that the week

was a disaster. Being only a year old she slept most of the time, and when she finally did wake up she wasn't allowed on the rides anyway, because she failed the minimum height restriction. The point was that by going to EuroDisney Shannon had got her own way and as far as she was concerned that gave her the green light to try and get her own way again … and again … and again … and again.

From that moment onwards Shannon Shellfish shouted **'I want!'** a thousand times a day, and because she always got what she wanted, she started to believe that the words were magic!

* * *

This is how it went most days in the Shellfish family.

Imagine a perfect scene around the supper table. Shannon has shepherd's pie and sprouts on her plate. Mr Shellfish has shepherd's pie and sprouts on his plate. Mrs Shellfish has shepherd's pie on her plate and is *adding* the sprouts — to be exact, they are in mid-air, on the serving spoon betwixt bowl and plate.

Now, not wanting her mother to have anything that she doesn't have, Shannon waits for the last sprout to roll on to her mother's plate before howling, 'I want that sprout!'

Naturally enough, Mrs Shellfish laughs at her daughter's ridiculous request and says, 'It's on my plate now, Shannon.'

This, however, does not put Shannon off. **'But I want it!'** she bawls, and goes on in a similar vein for five loud minutes until finally her father cracks.

'Just let her have it!' he cries. 'It's only a sprout!' So the sprout is lifted off the mother's plate and relocated to Shannon's, where it sits for a good ten minutes until Shannon makes an announcement.

'Ugh!' she says. 'It's cold. Don't want it now.'

This, in a nutshell, was the problem. Whatever Shannon wanted was always wasted. The truth was she didn't really want anything – except to be the boss and make her parents run around after her.

Time for another song . . .

Snip snap.
Clickety clack.
Bubble. trouble.
Hell and back!

You'll find out what it means in a minute.
Isn't it exciting! Just the thought of finding
out gets me frothing!

Birthdays always brought out the worst in
Shannon and her eleventh one was no
exception.

**'I want it! I want it! I want it! I
want it!'** They were passing a
pet shop at the time.

'Want what, dear?' said her
mother.

'A pet!' screamed Shannon.
'Something. I don't care.
Anything. Everything. That dog –
there.' She pointed to a puppy in a
basket. It had black rings around its eyes
like sunglasses.

'You want *that* dog?' Mr Shellfish sighed wearily.

'Yes. That dog for my birthday present. **I want it really badly!**' So they went inside.

Before they bought the puppy, however, Mr and Mrs Shellfish were extremely sensible and said all the right things. 'You will look after it, won't you?' her mother said and her father added, 'A dog is for life not just for your birthday.'

Shannon nodded in all the right places and convinced her parents and the pet shop owner that she was mature and responsible enough to look after another life. But when she got the dog home, it stained her favourite duvet brown and wiped its face on her flannel. So she chucked it in a skip.

Any normal parents would have handed in their child to the police or sent them on a long holiday to the salt mines of Siberia . . .

H
E
E
E
E
E
E
E
L
P
!

… but not Mr and Mrs Shellfish. Numbnuts that they were, they asked Shannon what she'd like instead! For once, Shannon did not know. She sat at the kitchen table and pondered the wish list in her head. She had just narrowed it down to a pony or cash, when the fickle pincer of fate rang the doorbell.

✳ ✳ ✳

When Shannon opened the door she got the shock of her life. Standing on the step was the largest lobster she had ever seen. It stood seven feet tall on its tail, and above its head it was snapping its huge pincers like a Flamenco dancer playing the maracas. It was a magnificent mutation that was, as it turned out, not real.

'Hubble, bubble, boil and trouble,' said Mr Pecorino, the Italian man inside the suit. 'I just open a new restaurant in the town.' He handed Shannon a printed leaflet. 'Please to come and bring your friends.'

'What's it called?' asked Shannon, eyeing the lobster suit closely.

'Hubble Bubble Boil and Trouble. I just tell you. We make very good lobsters.'

'That's what I want!' exploded Shannon so suddenly that the man in the lobster suit thought he had trodden on her toe.

'Sorry,' he said. 'I don't know how big my own tail is.'

'MUMMY!'

Shannon's mother came running. 'Yes, dear.'

'I know what I want for my birthday.'

'Can't it wait, dear? I'm icing your cake.'

'I want that lobster costume.' This was the first time Mrs Shellfish had noticed the seven-foot lobster standing outside her front door.

'Oh,' she said.

'Good afternoon,' said the lobster, extending a pincer of friendship. 'Mr Pecorino. Hubble Bubble Boil and Trouble. Please to come along and taste our lobsters.'

'Well?' interrupted Shannon. 'What are you waiting for, Mummy? Get the suit off him!'

Mrs Shellfish wasn't sure she should. 'The nice man probably needs it, dear.'

'But I WANT it!' howled her daughter.

Mr Pecorino had heard enough, besides he'd wasted too much time already. 'OK. I go now. Bye bye.'

But Shannon always got what she wanted. 'NOT SO FAST!' she yelled, diving full length across the front step to rugby tackle the lobster to the ground.

'Help!' cried Mr Pecorino, who lay stranded on his back like a beetle. 'What you do?'

'I want your lobster costume!' screamed Shannon.

Mr Pecorino had never been spoken to like this by a child before. 'Have no one ever told you, signorina . . .

'I WANT NEVER GETS!'

'Yes, it does,' said Shannon, grabbing something off the grass and sitting on the lobster's chest. 'Or I'll poke your eyes out with this sharp stick.'

'OK. OK. I listen!' Mr Pecorino was noted for his lobster, not his bravery. 'Here's the deal. You come to my restaurant tonight, eat my lobsters, pay my bill and you can have the suit. That way, *I* win and *you* win.'

'If you're lying,' hissed Shannon, leaning down and whispering in the lobster's ear, 'I'll find you. Only the stick I'll bring with me won't be sharp like this one. It'll be blunt. So more pain in the eyeballs. OK?'

'I not lie!' squealed Mr Pecorino, struggling to get away. There was a loud crack and he stopped dead. 'Owwww!' he cried. 'I think you break my tail.'

> Gurgle! Goo-goo!

> Who's there? Is that you, Garth? I thought I told you to stay in your room until you'd had your nappy changed

* * *

Shannon's parents pointed out to Shannon that in order to fulfil her side of the bargain she had to eat lobster.

'So?' she said.

'And you're happy with that?' asked her father.

'Why?'

'Because you don't like lobster,' said her mother.

'Not bothered,' said Shannon.

'Well, you should be,' said Mr Shellfish. 'You can't cook a lobster then *not* eat it.'

'Oh dear, how rude of me!' jeered Shannon all of a sudden. 'I didn't see the door open and the world expert on lobsters come into the room. In case you need reminding, Daddy, I can do anything I want.'

Her father lowered his voice to a growl. 'You obviously don't know why lobsters turn red when they're cooked,' he said.

'Are you trying to scare me?' mocked his daughter. 'Well, you're not succeeding, because I still want a lobster costume!'

'They turn red, because they're furious at being boiled alive,' he explained.

'They have terrible tempers,' cried Mrs Shellfish. 'When they're angry their pincers go snip, snip! Snip, snip, snip! Snip ...'

But Shannon wasn't impressed. What harm could a teeny-tiny lobster do to *her*?

'You're not listening,' she said. Then she screamed until the veins in her forehead stood out like knotted string. 'It's my birthday and **I want a lobster costume.** OK?'

When her super-soft parents agreed to her demands, it was a huge relief to me, because if they hadn't she would never have ended up in the soup... lobster bisque, of course!

Now that she was going out to a posh restaurant for her birthday, Shannon had a whole new list of *wants*. First up, she wanted a new dress.

'But you already have hundreds of new dresses in your wardrobe,' gasped her mother. 'I bought you a new one every week last year and you never wear them.'

'I've never been this old before, have I?' said Shannon. 'Those dresses were bought for a younger girl. Besides, this is a special occasion and I want to wow the crowds outside the restaurant!'

'Crowds!' tittered her father. 'There won't be any crowds.'

'Then get me some!' came the order. 'For once in my life, **I want to feel special!**'

So her father contacted Rent-A-Crowd and organised a welcoming party while her mother took her to the shops to buy that dress. Only when they got there it wasn't just one dress . . .

'They're *all* so beautiful!' Shannon cried, snatching three off one rail and adding them to the pile of mohair in her mother's arms.

'**I want this!** And this! And this! And that! And these!' She jumped onto a mannequin's plinth and made a sweeping gesture across the boutique. '**I want everything I can see!**'

But when they got outside, Shannon went off the lot and dumped them in a skip. Right on top of a puppy, as it happened.

'Ugh!' she sneered. 'Wouldn't be seen dead in those!'

Her mother pursued her up the street and asked her what she would be seen dead in, but Shannon didn't know. 'We'll just have to go on until I find something I want,' she said.

> I always recommend a shroud for being seen dead in. It's what every corpse is wearing this year!

> Oink! Oink!

> Apart from Truffle. obviously. He's wearing pig skin.

They tried on a mile of dresses, but none was quite right. As far as Shannon was concerned they were variously too long, too short, too black, too brown, too low, too high, too feathery, too frumpy, too flowing or too nice. It took her mother calling a dress 'Too much!' to bring Shannon to a decision.

'**But I WANT this one!**' she cried. 'It's my birthday! How can you put a price on your precious daughter's happiness?' It was inevitable that Shannon would want the most expensive. Mrs Shellfish handed over her credit card with a squirm of embarrassment.

'Charge it up,' she said.

Now that the dress was sorted, the next thing Shannon wanted was a white limousine. At least she did until it was booked and then she wanted something else.

'I can't go to a swanky restaurant in a boring old limousine,' she said. '**I want to go in a helicopter.** And when I arrive I want the crowd to be cheering. I want someone to open my door, I want a red carpet, I want lights, I want fanfares, I want the crowd to the press lined up with their cameras, and I want a choir of sweet little schoolboys singing *Hallelujah!*' She stared at her parents. 'What?!'

They stared back as if she'd taken leave of her senses.

'What's wrong?'

'Will there be anything else?' mocked Mr Shellfish. His daughter spat back like a snake.

'Don't be sarcastic, Daddy. It's not clever.' And Daddy being Daddy, Daddy did as he was told.

I want Shannon to get everything she's ever wanted and not check in to The Hothell Darkness so I can tease the badness out of her! Oh dear. I just remembered. 'I want never gets!' What a pity. I'll just have to give her a room after all!

⁕ ⁕ ⁕

The night unfolded as expected. Shannon's parents knew that their daughter would reject everything she'd asked for, and sure enough she did.

Before they'd even left home she clumped down the stairs in her new long evening gown and with a cry of **'I want it shorter!'**, tore a strip off the bottom until it was a miniskirt. She felt sick in the helicopter, so pulled off the pilot's headphones and bellowed, **'I want to walk!'** She grew tired of the rented crowds outside the restaurant and sent them packing with a shriek of **'I want to be alone!'** And in the restaurant itself, she ordered the largest lobster in the tank . . . and then refused to eat it.

'I don't *want* lobster!' she screamed when Mr Pecorino placed the plate down in front of her. Mr Shellfish thought he'd made himself clear on the question of not leaving lobster and firmly corrected his daughter's manners.

'I'm sorry, Shannon, but you've ordered it, you have to eat it.'

'Don't want to,' she sulked.

Mr Pecorino had stopped smiling. 'But it is cooked now!' he said firmly. 'You *must* eat it or the lobster he die for nothing.' Shannon pushed the plate away from her.

'I don't do what other people want me to do, Mr

Lobster–Man. I only do what I want to do, **and I want my present!** OK?!'

'I thought we have a deal,' growled Mr Pecorino. 'Eat first, costume later.'

'Then you thought wrong,' replied the girl, 'because I hate lobster! It makes me sick!'

'Oh dear,' trembled Mrs Shellfish, screwing the corners of her napkin into the cooked lobster's ears. 'I do hope it can't hear you.'

But of course it could. And the more the lobster heard, the crosser it became. Lobsters are very similar to human beings. They're not that keen on being boiled alive for no good reason.

Meanwhile, Shannon had left the table and chased Mr Pecorino into the kitchen, where she had picked up a wooden spoon and was once again threatening to poke his eyes out unless he gave her what she wanted. He showed her the cupboard where he kept the lobster costume and left her to climb into it.

In the restaurant, however, the unwanted cooked lobster had reached the end of its tether. Steam rose from its shell as it gestured angrily to its live friends in the tank by the window. It stood on its red tail and clicked its pincers above its head like an angry tic-tac man. The effect was instantaneous. The live lobsters formed a lobster ladder in the water and climbed over each other's backs until they could reach the lip of the tank. Then they threw themselves out onto the floor. Other diners stood up quickly and rushed into the street before the tide of pincers pinched them. The floor was heaving with black crustaceans, moving like an oil slick towards the kitchen door.

Just then Shannon emerged from the kitchen wearing the lobster costume.

'I want someone to zip me up!' she announced to the empty room. The lack of diners came as something of a shock.

'Shannon!' shouted Mrs Shellfish.

'Walk towards us now!' cried her father. 'And don't look down!'

But nobody *ever* told Shannon what to do!

The moment she looked down, however, she wished she hadn't. It was like looking into a bottomless black sea. The lobsters swarmed over her feet and up her legs and body. They knocked her onto her back and picked her up in their pincers.

'What are you doing?' she yelled. **'I want you to stop. I want to get down!'**

But too many years of being pushed around by humans have made lobsters immune to such pleadings. With cold, armour-plated fury they scuttled into the kitchen where a large pot of water was still on the boil. Then they passed her over their heads towards the bubbling.

'No!' she yelled. 'No! I don't want to go in there! No! It's hot! Eeeeyooooooooooooooow!'

And that was the first and last time that a lobster has ever screamed.

She's screamed quite a lot since, though!

Oh for goodness' sake! Does Monty never shut up?

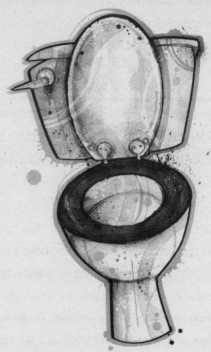

Who's that shouting out now? There's never a
moment's peace in this hothell. I love it because it
means I'm doing something right! Oh. I might have
guessed. Room 492.572. The Crybaby! He hasn't
stopped complaining since his soul showed up last
month. There wasn't much of him left apart from
his soul. He had half a lip and one thumb, as I
recall, which he was still sucking.

NEXT AN INTERESTING FACT

Because I know everything, I know that you will be extremely happy when you move in here.

> Don't listen to the nasty big man! Gurgle! Goo, goo! He's an ickle liar!

His name is Garth MacQueen, a boy for whom the term 'nasty little beast' might have been invented. His story starts as far back as the seventeenth century, when babies living in the Scottish Highlands were snatched by wild wolves and devoured in the woods like flightless chickens!

In 1743, the last of the wild wolves was killed by a man called Eagan MacQueen — notice the same last name. It was Eagan MacQueen who cut off the beast's head and gave it to his

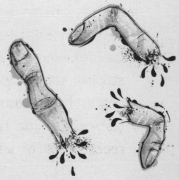

wife to put in the pot. But as the stock boiled and the head slowly rolled in the upsurge of bubbles, the wild wolf's steel-grey eyes swivelled in their sockets and drank in one last look at their destroyer before clouding over for good.

Eagan MacQueen had been eyeballed. The wild wolf's revenge was astir. It would, however, be THREE HUNDRED YEARS before it came to completion.

It was well worth waiting for, though!

WOLF CHILD

Living on the edge of the Darnaway Forest were the wolf slayer's descendants: Elspet and Callum MacQueen, their son Garth, and newborn baby, Moira. Their house was on a modern estate built on top of the spot where Eagan MacQueen had stewed the wolf's head.

The residents were nervous. There had been unconfirmed sightings of wild wolves in the forest, which the police had dismissed as superstitious nonsense. Then a gillie had died hunting stags and a grandmother picnicking with her grandchildren had seen their roast chicken taken off by a 'beast with steel-grey eyes'. Such stories fuelled rumours that the wild wolves had returned, and with them came fear. The crash of a dustbin lid or the squeak of an unlocked gate in the middle of the night was enough to make grown men sit up in their beds and quiver.

'We must take great care with the new

baby,' said Callum at supper one night. Moira
was only a week old and had just come home
from the hospital. 'Never let her out of your
sight, Elspet, for the wolves need only a
moment to snatch her.'

'Is it true about the wild wolves coming
back?' asked Garth. 'Are they living in the
garden?'

Callum chuckled. 'Nay, son. There's nothing
to bother yourself about. 'Tis only the wee
babies they take.'

'You mean Moira?' Garth gasped with horror.
'They might take my baby sister?' Then quite
suddenly, his look of concern burst into an evil
grin. 'Cool,' he said. 'Bring them on!'

✹ ✹ ✹

Garth had a problem with his baby sister. He
didn't like her. Ever since she'd arrived nobody
had paid him any attention. When his
mother had brought the baby home,
Garth had greeted her at the front door.
He had stood there with his arms
outstretched for a kiss, but she
hadn't seen him and had knocked
him down with her knee. And now
if he wanted her to read him a book

at bedtime, he had to push Moira off his mother's lap while the baby was feeding. It was as if Garth had become invisible. Maybe, he thought, watching his mother and father fawning over Moira in the bath, if he behaved like a baby his parents would start noticing him again.

'Actually, that's not a bad idea,' he muttered to himself.

It wasn't a bad idea. It was a DREADFUL idea! But not in a way that Garth could ever have predicted

From that day on, Garth behaved like a baby. At lunchtime, he sucked his thumb on the bus and cried when his mother slapped the back of his hand.

'Oh cruel, Mummy! Waaaaaah!' he wailed in his baby voice. 'Why you no let baby sucky thumb?'

His mother looked at him askance. 'What sort of language is that for a ten year old?'

The language of control, thought Garth. It

wraps you round my little finger. He didn't say it out loud, obviously, in case she had a blue fit.

✹ ✹ ✹

Later, in the supermarket, he insisted on being carried and, when his mother said no, he stopped in the aisle, dug in his heels and refused to move until she did as she was told!

'Behave, Garth!' A mother does not take orders from her own son.

'But baby am tired, Mumsy-wumsy. Me wanna sit on your shoulder-woulders.'

'No!'

'Garthy am wanna sleepy-byes.'

'Stop talking like a baby.' When his mother raised her voice that meant she was losing her cool, and that meant it was time to turn the emotional screw. It was time for baby to howl!

'Waaaaaah!' he screeched. 'Mumsy-wumsy's cross with me! Waaaaaah!'

'Garth!' she hissed, as all eyes turned to stare. 'Stop that! Everyone's looking!' When his mother hissed with embarrassment it was all over; game set and match to Garth.

'Carry me, then,' he gloated with

outstretched arms and a scheming smile.

At dinner that night he threw a tantrum. He hurled his plate at his parents and covered them with half-chewed carrots and potatoes.

'Baby don't like vegetables!' he screamed. 'It's pooh!'

And at three o'clock in the morning, with a light drizzle falling outside, he woke his parents up by climbing into their bed with a pillowcase full of toys.

'Me and my toys is scared of the tunder and lighting!' he lied, emptying the contents of the pillowcase on top of his parents' heads. 'Oh, Mumsy-wumsy, what's wrong? Why is yous crying?'

'You've just dropped a car on the bridge of her nose!' fumed Mr MacQueen. 'Now act your age, Garth, and go back to bed!' But this only had one effect.

'Dadda's shouting at baby! Waaaaaah!'

❋ ❋ ❋

The next day he strawberry jammed the kitchen wallpaper, painting a gruesome picture of wild wolves gobbling up a little girl. He showed it to Moira and grinned with cruel delight.

'That's not jam coming from the ickle sister's head!' he said. 'That's blood! And that ickle sister's *you*!' His tone was so viperous that her bottom lip began to wobble. 'And there's blood all over, because you is DEAD!' Moira burst into tears and didn't stop for two days.

Then, on Thursday, he was sick in the car. Not once but twice, and both without warning.

'Oops! Sorry, Dadda.'

'Why didn't you tell me you felt unwell?' protested his father who had got every last drop of stomach-soup down his neck.

'I'm a baby,' said Garth. 'I don't know how to stop myself.'

His father slammed on the brakes and got out to clean himself up. 'I don't know what's got into you, Garth.'

'I think what got into me was all this chocolate what I ate,' he grinned, showing his father the empty wrapper off a half-kilo bar of Dairy Delight.

'I don't mean that,' snapped his father. 'I mean all this baby stuff. If you don't grow up quick, son, the baby-bolting wolves will be coming for *you*!'

'Ooh, I am scared,' mocked Garth. 'Double up my nappy!'

But he should have been scared for the forest had ears. As they drove on along the road that bisected Darnaway Forest, a pair of steel-grey eyes swivelled in their sockets and followed the path of the car. A grey tail twitched in the undergrowth and a rough, pink tongue scraped along slavering lips.

I'll let you into a secret. It wasn't me!

It was Garth MacQueen's turn to be eyeballed.

❋ ❋ ❋

That night, Garth had a terrible dream. In his dream he was asleep in bed, when a knock at the door awakened him. Confident that it could only be his parents outside, he wound them up by crying out like a baby.

'Mamma, Dadda! Me is so scared of the big

bad wolf. Baby Garfy want a cuddle! Mamma, Dadda! Come and save your baby Garfy!'

The door handle turned slowly, leading Garth to believe that his parents were doing as they were told and coming in to save him. He cried out to encourage them. 'Goo-goo. Gaga. Goo-g . . .'

But the childish noises stuck in his throat when, instead of his parents, four wild wolves slunk through the door.

'No, no!' he yelled. 'I'm not a baby really. I'm ten years old. I'm nearly a man. I only did it to get attention from my Mummy and Daddy, but I'll stop now. I will. Please! If you're hungry you can take my sister instead. She's a *real* baby. No. She is! No. Go away!'

But the wild wolves weren't going anywhere without their prize. They stopped by the side of the bed, picked their teeth with their razor-sharp claws, leered like a gang of cut-throats and pounced. Garth struggled, but could not escape their crushing jaws. He felt their hard teeth sink through his flesh and bruise his bones; he smelled their rank breath; he stared deep into their cold, grey eyes and saw himself reflected there, floppy and limp like a lifeless baby.

Then he woke up, screaming. As he sat up in the dark and panted with fear, Garth vowed never to behave like a baby again. What if the wild wolves came while he was *pretending* to be a baby? Instead of Moira, they might snatch *him*! He was ten years old and from now on he *was* going to act his age; every day of every week of every month of every year! He was giving up baby for good!

> Unfortunately, it was an ickle bit late for that!

Outside the window, a metal dustbin rolled noisily across the mud and banged against a wire fence. In front of a hole in this fence a freshly-made paw print glistened in the moonlight, and above it, snagged on the bent barbed wire, was a warm clump of grey fur. Garth saw none of these, nor noticed the tiny puncture mark on his arm still wet with wolf spit. Maybe his dream had not been a dream after all.

✼ ✼ ✼

Early the next morning, when Garth swung his legs over the side of the mattress to get out of bed, he received a nasty surprise. His feet didn't touch the floor. In fact, his feet were rushing up to meet him. His legs were getting shorter! He knocked the side of his head with the heel of his hand to wake himself up, but he wasn't asleep. He jumped down off his bed and his feet landed in his slippers which were six sizes too big.

'What's going on?' he puzzled, as he ran across the wide open space that now separated the bed from the basin. The space had grown. And when he arrived at the basin to brush his teeth he was too small to see over the rim. This was no joke. Garth threw a skipping rope over the back of a chair and pulled himself up onto the seat. If he stood on his tiptoes he could just see the top of his head in the mirror. There was no doubt about it. He was shrinking!

No joking this time. Garth needed his mummy and daddy NOW!

'Help!' he screamed. 'Help! Mummy! Daddy! Save me!' But his words bubbled out as a string of gurgle and spit.

He rolled off the chair and hit the floor hard. No matter. He would reach the door, open it, let himself out and find his parents. But he couldn't stand up. He couldn't walk. His legs weren't strong enough. So he *crawled* to the door, stumbling twice on his weak elbows, but when he stretched up for the handle, it was out of his reach. 'Mummy! Daddy!'

In their bedroom, Garth's parents only heard a baby's cry. 'Gurgle! Goo-goo!'

'Is that Garth?' sighed Mrs MacQueen, rubbing her eyes and shaking herself awake.

'Ignore the selfish boy,' said her husband. 'He's just seeking attention again.'

Which was why Garth's parents ignored him all the next day, when he lay on his back in his bedroom and screamed and screamed, and wet his trousers. He only stopped screaming when his mother stuck a dummy in his mouth.

Gurgle! Goo-g—

But the day after that, when Garth's teeth and hair fell out during tea, his parents started to worry.

'You're not acting any more, are you?' said Mr MacQueen fearfully.

'Gurgle! Goo-goo!' replied Garth.

'Something happened that night to change you.'

'Gurgle! Goo-goo!'

'Oh, Callum, no!' cried Garth's mother. 'Don't you see… the shrinking, the talking, the toothless gums! It's wolf-witchery. He really *has* turned into a baby!'

The descendants of Eagan MacQueen heard a lupine howl outside and both blanched.

'*Moira!*' Elspet had left their other baby in the pram in the garden! 'I put her outside for some fresh air!'

Mr and Mrs MacQueen rushed out of the house, leaving Garth alone in the front room, lying on a blanket, chewing on a rusk. They stumbled into the garden, expecting to find their beautiful baby girl flopped in the jaws of a child-chomping wolf, but the pram was exactly where Elspet had left it. Moira was safe. Then, at exactly the same moment Elspet and Callum had exactly the same thought.

'Garth!' she gasped, her face etched with terror. 'They've got in behind us!'

'What have we done?' he howled. 'I told him not to behave like a baby. What did I say? If he didn't grow up quick, the wolves would come for *him*! But he wouldn't listen. HE WOULDN'T LISTEN!'

They rushed back into the front room, but the wild wolves had outsmarted them. In the twinkling of a steel-grey eye, they had exacted their three-hundred-year revenge. Wild wolves are cunning creatures who hunt in packs. While one wolf howled a distraction in the back garden, tearing the parents away from their baby son, another slipped in through the open front window and snatched baby Garth by the nape of his neck.

And that was that. Nobody has seen Garth since. It is thought that the wild wolves took him into Darnaway Forest, but what happened after that is a mystery.

I don't think it is, really. Wolf-baby. Baby-wolf. Think about it. There's not much doubt in my mind. They don't share a common love of sport or cinema, do they? They can't discuss politics or go to the pub for a pint and a sandwich. No, I think we all know what happened. The wolves ate him. And jolly tasty he probably was too. Nice and plump.

> ## Gurgle! Goo-goo!

Oh! They had him with mustard, apparently.

The best baby recipe I know is Hawaiian Baby, which is ridiculously simple. All you need is a barbecue, a grass skirt and a tin of pineapple chunks. And a baby, of course.

Ooh, I tell you what I've never tried and might be nice: baby burgers. There was a time when the bat in Room 493.111 would have liked those.

THE FRUIT BAT

Once upon a Turkey Twizzler, there lived a girl called Cherie Stone, which was an odd name for a girl who hated fruit. Instead of eating food that was good for her, she stuffed her face with sugary sweets and saturated fats: burgers, pizzas, chocolate, chips and fizzy pop. It did terrible things to her body. It blocked up her insides like a double dose of cement and meant that for the best part of a year she couldn't go to the loo. With nothing getting out, but plenty going in, she grew and grew and grew and grew until she was too big to fit in the smallest room in the house (not that she ever needed to go in there) and looked like a giant potato.

What did you just say? Yes you! WHAT IS A POTATO? You are putting my tail, aren't you?

You don't know what a potato looks like?

'Hello thickos! Anybody home?'

If you're that ignorant maybe I don't want you down here. Actually, no. Cancel that. I can always find a use for you in the Bloodletting Room as a bit of old rag to mop up with!

Next - an interesting fact

NEXT - AN INTERESTING FACT

For those of you who know nothing, the potato was brought back from South America by Sir Walter Raleigh in 1588. That means, peasants in William Shakespeare's day knew what a potato looked like. Even goats can describe a potato – at least they could if they could speak. A potato is sort of round and dirty with eyes where the weevils have burrowed.

Cherie Stone looked like a potato, because her bowels were bunged up. To get things moving, Mr and Mrs Stone took their daughter to the doctor, a shrew-faced Scottish man with a strong Glaswegian accent and bright red hair. He measured Cherie's girth and weighed her in a horse's harness before delivering his diagnosis.

'At's constipation,' he said gravely. 'Forty-thud case thus wick.'

'But what can we do?' asked Mrs Stone. 'She's so heavy I couldn't bring her on the bus.'

The doctor sat back in his chair and thought deeply. Finally, he leaned forward and offered his prescription. 'If ya wunt to poosh it oot, thar's noot as good as froot!'

So fruit it was.

Hang on. I'm twitching again. You do know what fruit is, don't you? OH COME ON! You must have seen it soft, sweet and squidgy; livens up a smoothie; tops off an ice cream? So you have seen it. Good.

But do you eat it? If you do, CURSES! You will lead a long and happy life. If you don't you'll be coming down here to live with me. So please, DON'T START EATING FRUIT NOW. And when you're NOT eating fruit promise me that you'll open your bedroom window and shout out:

'I DON'T EAT FRUIT!' because then THEY will hear you! Hanging upside down off a branch, their ears will twitch and they'll hear you scream that there's fruit in your house that is NOT being eaten! And once they know that, you are doomed! And once you are doomed you are MINE! Because they will come, in the middle of the night. You will wake to the sound of snapping teeth and a long flicky tongue sucking all the juice out! And that's what I want. So don't eat fruit. Don't even look at it. Be bad. Be mine.

Oink! Oink!

Alternatively, be bacon stuffing.

Anyway, we'll save that for later. For the time being, let's get back to that stupid doctor (I hate doctors always interfering and making children BETTER!) telling Cherie to save her life by eating more fruit.

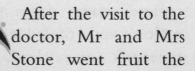

After the visit to the doctor, Mr and Mrs Stone went fruit the loop. They dressed up in large gooseberry cotumes and threatened to kiss their daughter outside her school gates if she didn't eat fruit. So embarrassed was Cherie at the sight of her parents puckering in green tights that she changed schools and didn't tell them. Her parents stood outside her old school for a week until the police arrested them and confiscated their costumes.

At home, they hid fruit around the house, in every nook and cranny, so that it was always available to tempt their bulging daughter into a fruity nibble. They draped grapes over the shower head in the bathroom to lure her during her ablutions; they filled her wardrobe with oranges and grapefruit to bombard her when she opened the doors; they decorated the apples and pears with apples and pears; they replaced the furry dice on the rear view mirror of the car with furry kiwi fruit; they swapped door handles for bananas, the TV remote control for a slice of melon, and the dog for a pineapple on a lead, which caused untold problems when Cherie walked it past a greengrocer's and the pineapple got into a fight with a pawpaw. Yet despite her parents' ingenuity and invention, Cherie's interest in fruit remained fixed at zero.

✹ ✹ ✹

So Mr and Mrs Stone came up with a cunning plan. Reasoning that it was Cherie's *daytime* brain that vetoed the fruit, they decided to use her *sleeptime* brain to change her mind. They secretly sewed miniature speakers into her pillows, and when she went to sleep at night they played her tapes of the sound of luscious loganberries growing in the Scottish Lowlands, and succulent strawberries blossoming in Shard. Their idea was to reshape her dreams in a fruit-ward direction so that when she woke up the only thing she thought about was fruit!

And it worked – nearly.

Her brain created fruity landscapes in her dreams: a bright yellow lemon shone over coconut hills, while a banana punt floated down an orange juice river full of peachy fish and plum frogs. But no sooner had this fruit appeared in her dreams than the anti-fruit side of Cherie's brain invented squadrons of giant wasps that ate all the fruit and put a stop to the brainwashing.

Cherie Stone hated fruit and *nothing* was ever going to get her to eat it.

That's NOTHING as in SOMETHING that goes squeak! squeak! splat!

She still had the problem of getting her parents off her back, however. If only she could convince them that eating fruit was dangerous, maybe they would stop begging her to eat it.

It took her several days of brain-wracking to come up with a story, but when she did it was a corker.

'You see,' she said at breakfast, 'I would eat fruit, but I can't.'

'You mean you won't,' sulked her mother.

'No, *can't*.' Cherie grinned slyly. She rearranged her features to look terrified. 'Because of the fruit bats!'

'What have fruit bats got to do with anything?' said Mrs Stone.

'Because fruit bats are attracted by the smell of fruit,' replied Cherie.

'I know that,' said her mother. 'So what's your point?'

'My point is that if a girl eats fruit, the smell of fruit in her stomach attracts the fruit bats who love fruit beyond all measure. And they come in the middle of the night, screeching out of a darkling sky to devour her. And she dies horribly in her bed, screaming while the bats eat her, chomping through her flesh to get at the fruit inside. And in the morning, parents generally come in and find the bits that are left strewn out across the bed clothes, which is really horrible too and makes the parents scream. And *then* a stalk grows out of the girl's remains – out of her head if she's still got one – and keeps on growing while she's buried in her coffin!'

'I didn't know that,' said her mother, clearly not believing a word.

'It's true,' persisted Cherie. 'I read it in a kids' magazine called *Dead Fruit Eaters' Weekly*, which has got stories about all the millions of children who die from fruit related deaths every week!'

Her mother gasped and feigned concern. 'You're not going to die are you?' she said.

'I might do,' said Cherie, lowering her eyes to look pathetic, 'if you make me eat fruit.'

'Oh well,' said her mother, dropping all pretence at distress, 'at least you'll die healthy.' And she tossed a grape across the table for Cherie to catch.

'You don't believe me, do you?' said Cherie indignantly, as the grape bounced off her shoulder and fell to the floor.

'No. I've never heard such tummy rot in all my life! Fruit bats don't eat children.'

'Yeah well, they *do* actually,' shrieked Cherie, getting up from the table. 'So you can carry on buying fruit as much as you like, but it'll just go to rot, because I won't eat fruit. Never! Do you hear me?' Then she flounced out of the kitchen, slapping her father's newspaper on the way. When she reached the doorway she turned her vast bulk around to have the last word. 'You'll be sorry when I'm dead!' she bawled, and then she was gone, squeezing through the door and slamming it behind her.

'Not sure I will,' said Mr Stone.

I'm sure I won't!

What Cherie didn't know was that fruit bats have incredibly sensitive hearing. Nearby in the branches of a codling tree, when Cherie spoke the words 'So you can carry on buying fruit as much as you like, but it'll just go to rot, because I won't eat fruit. Never!' a pair of pointed ears stood rigidly to attention. Cherie was right about something; Fruit bats live for fruit. They love it more than life itself. So when this particular Fruit bat heard that fruit was going to waste, it had no choice but to find the fruit and eat it first. And that meant setting a course for Cherie Stone.

Half an hour later, Cherie Stone was walking to school when she found a banana in her rucksack. Her mother had hidden it under her gym kit just in case her daughter suddenly felt peckish after netball. As Cherie tossed it into a bin the sound of a twig snapping close by made her freeze. She sneaked a glance over her shoulder to see if she was being followed.

'Hello,' she called out. 'Hello. Who's there?' Nobody replied.

Later, in the school dining hall, when Cherie opened her packed lunch box she found a peach. Her mother had lovingly sliced it and sneaked it in under her marshmallow sandwich. As she took the peach out to leave it on her plate, she heard a scuffling in the roof beams above her. She looked up, but there was nothing there.

And later still, on her way home from school, when she found a stupid kumquat in her pocket ... there it was again! That feeling that she was being watched. That something was out there, waiting to pounce. She threw the kumquat away and broke into a slow trot, to get home as quickly as she could.

Had she turned around Cherie would have seen a shadow with long, thin grasshopper legs scuttle out from behind a bush. She would also have seen a brown beast on the wing streak through the air and land with a squelch on the kumquat. It plunged its sharp teeth into the heart of the fruit and tore out the flesh like a jackal!

For supper Cherie Stone's mother had cooked upside-down pudding with raspberries on top, but Cherie stared out of the window and ate crisps instead.

'Did anyone else just see a shadow out there?' she asked nervously.

'If you're still trying to make me believe your silly fruit bat story, Cherie, forget it! Fruit bats do *not* eat little girls. There is *not* one in the garden. I do *not* believe you!' Her mother had lost her temper. 'You'll say anything to get out of eating fruit. Now, start your pudding.'

'No,' said her hulking daughter, leaving the room with a chocolate bar in her hand. 'Not hungry.'

And so to bed. To the reinforced bed custom-built by a bridge engineer to support Cherie's vast weight. She eased herself under the duvet and ate the bar of chocolate. Then she turned off the light, rolled onto her back and closed her eyes.

And so to sleep. *for the very last time!*

On her way to bed, Cherie's mother did what she did every night. She placed a tangerine on Cherie's pillow, in case her daughter should be woken by the ache of an empty stomach. But on this particular night, for no particular reason, she hesitated by the side of the bed and as a little afterthought, popped a plum in the pocket of Cherie's pyjamas – just above her daughter's pumping heart! Then she left the room and went to bed herself.

✳ ✳ ✳

By midnight, Cherie was asleep. This meant that she didn't hear the noise at the window; the noise that sounded like the flapping of a shroud. The fruit bat landed on the ledge outside, pulled open the window with its claw, sniffed the air for fruit and stepped inside. It dropped to the floor with a thump, lurched across the wooden floorboards on its knuckles, hopped onto the bed and drew its wrinkled face level with Cherie's. It only wanted to eat the tangerine and then it would go. But once the tangerine had been devoured, its sensitive nose picked up another scent. The smell of something even sweeter and juicier; the smell of a real treat – the plum in Cherie Stone's pocket!

With mouth agape and gnashers glinting, the fruit bat lunged to take the plum, but the pocket was made from thick flannelette which muddled the fruit bat's radar. It lost its bearings and lunged too fast and too far, biting not only through the plum's skin, but through into Cherie's heart as well! Cherie opened her eyes and screamed as a spurt of bright-red blood hit the ceiling above her head. And then it was over. The blackness descended as the Fruit bat retired through the window and flew back to its codling tree having gorged on the fruit; flesh, juice, *stone* and all!

When Cherie Stone woke up she didn't know where she was and wondered why she wasn't in bed any more. Her head felt like it was going to

burst, as if it was full of
blood and still filling. Her
feet felt strange too. The
muscles ached from gripping.
She heard voices below her and opened her eyes
to find that she was hanging off a branch. The
world was upside down.

'Look, it's woken up!' came the cry. She
peered down and saw three children standing
below her. She noticed too that she was holding
a codling apple in her hand and her mouth had
filled with water. There was nothing in the
world she wanted *more*. She took a bite and
licked her lips. It was delicious!

'Kill it!' shouted the little boy, hurling a stone
at Cherie's head. 'Knock it out the tree.'

The stone hit her on the gripping leg
and dislodged her claw. 'Help!' she cried
as she plunged towards the ground, but
her body knew what it was doing. As
her wings unfurled she pulled out of
the dive and Cherie realised what had
happened. An accidental bite to the heart
had turned her into a Fruit bat! Unfortunately
there was no time to dwell on her misfortune,
because the children were still throwing rocks at

her. She was still not out of danger. If they hit her and brought her down, they would stamp on her tiny head and burst her brains to billio! What could she do?

Luckily, that was when her tummy rumbled. *That* was when an unfamiliar gurgle bubbled in her gut and burst out behind her like an exploding slurry pit, shooting her into the sky with the force of a jet engine and showering her attackers in a noxious waterfall of stinking brown bat poo!

'Well, that was a bonus,' grinned the new slimmed-down bat-girl. After all, it had been the best part of a year since she'd been to the loo. Now, after eating just one codling apple, it was all systems go again. Then she turned due west and flew half way round the world into The Darkness.

I have my fun with her down here. Mainly at YOUR expense. I let her out sometimes to find some fruit. because it amuses me to think of someone like you underneath her when she eats a codling apple!

You do see what I mean. don't you?

Here's a word of warning: When Cherie's out and about don't leave home without an umbrella!

I should have known you wouldn't understand. If you don't know what a potato looks like how could I ever expect you to imagine a world where pedestrians are splattered in bat poo?

'HEEEEEEEEEEEEEEEELP!'

Oh not again. I thought he'd gone away. I wish that python would do us all a favour and just eat him!

If that doesn't shut him up
I don't know what will.

'Oy! Was that bat poo just went up my nose?'

'Might have been.' Haha! I love bats!

That's it. We've reached the end of our little journey through the Animal Wing. It will soon be time for you to wave goodbye to your old life and register with me. I hope these NASTY LITTLE BEASTS have taught you lots of new ways to be bad, because if they have it makes my job worthwhile.

There's one last story. It belongs to the child in Room 492.575. You can't miss it; it's the room that's been sealed with polythene to keep the smell in. The room is so filthy I've seen cockroaches packing their bags and leaving. It won't come as any surprise to you to know that the child inside is a BOY and his story is all about pigs . . .

What? What? WHAT?

No! Don't tell me you don't know what a pig looks like! A bit like a SAUSAGE only bigger, pinker, four more legs and bags more get up and go!

108

THE CLOTHES PIGS

This tale starts with a toasty-warm sunrise and a golden-fingered glow that creeps over the treetops and spills down the hill towards Cherry Tree Farm. It also starts with a full-throated cock crow and a rustling of sweet-smelling hay, with Gertude the duck and her fluffy little ducklings waddling across the farmyard, and with Daisy the cow nudging the stragglers to help them keep up. This tale starts with all the pretty animals on the pretty farm waking from a night of pretty dreams. There was Billy the goat, Roger the horse and Insy, Winsy, Nibble and Titch, the four little pink piglets. They were the smallest, sweetest, silliest little pink piglets

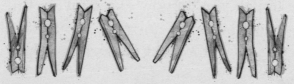

you ever did see and they were always getting into scrapes.

One day, for example, a solid sow called Bertha, who had taken up ballet to keep fit, was concentrating hard on getting her leg up onto the practice bar when the four little piglets tumbled into the sty playing catch tag. She didn't see them and accidentally trod on Insy. So startled was she by his squeal of pain that she lost her balance and crashed to the ground in a cloud of dust and giggles!

'Oh dear,' she cried, wiping tears of laughter from her eyes, 'I've seen ballet pumps bigger than you!'

It was true. When they were born Insy, Winsy, Nibble and Titch were no bigger than coffee beans, and because they never got any food they had barely grown at all. Their elder brothers and sisters had a way of reaching the slops first: shoulder barging, tail pulling, ear biting and kicking each other out of the way, to name but four. If you've ever seen pigs feeding at the trough you'll know exactly what I mean. It's a brutal business; noisy, ferociously blood-spattered and not a good manner in sight.

> A bit like a school-dinner queue!

But enough of the nasties. The point is that deprived of food Insy, Winsy, Nibble and Titch were permanently hungry, and hungry pigs have got to eat sometime. It's just a question of *when*, *how* and *who*.

> You mean, you didn't know that pigs in a feeding frenzy can eat a child whole without turning a bristle? I'm astonished. You've obviously never met the Clothes Pigs!

Close by to Cherry Tree Farm, in a big, smoky city unused to seeing pigs on the streets, there lived a misguided boy by the name of Truman Snuffle, or Truffle for short. Truffle was a slob of a child, who treated his home like a hotel and his parents like slaves. He made his father do all the heavy tasks around the house, such as carrying him up and down stairs, switching off his bedroom light or opening the toothpaste tube, while his mother did everything else. He never offered to clear up after she'd cooked him a meal. He never ran his own bath, or washed his own toes or made his own bed. He never changed his own channels on the telly, or turned his own keys in the front door, or put his own rubbish in the wastepaper bin. And he never (repeat *never*) picked up his own clothes. Clothes that his mother had spent hours washing, ironing, folding and putting away neatly in his cupboard, clothes that he chucked on the floor like a pig!

Appropriate that. a pig . . .

Truffle's bedroom looked like a pigsty. Actually, it wasn't *just* his bedroom. Piles of discarded clothes were dotted around the house like steaming heaps of elephant dung dotted around a grassy plain: outside the bathroom, by the back door, in the hall, on the stairs, down the back of the sofa; little surprises for Truffle's mother to find and deal with - sweaty socks, crumpled T-shirts, and old pants. Never a day passed when Truffle's parents did not beg him to pick up his clothes and never a day passed when Truffle did not reply, 'I'd like to *pick up* a new set of parents!'

'This can't go on!' wailed his mother. They were standing in his pit of a bedroom. 'You're wearing me out. I finish clearing up one mess only to find you making another!'

'You're my *mother*,' said Truffle imperiously. 'It is your *job* to clear up around me. That is why you have been put here on this earth, and the sooner you get used to it the easier it will be for both of us.'

'Steady on,' said Truffle's father, but Mrs Snuffle did not need his support, she had a game plan all of her own.

'If you continue to turn my house into a pigsty,' she bristled, 'the Clothes Pigs will pay you a visit.'

'The *what*?'

'The Clothes Pigs.' She unhooked a grey sock from the lampshade and lifted a shoe off the bedside table. 'They're little piggies who live in pig sties like this! They'll get rid of you and that will be that!' Truffle poured scorn on his mother's pathetic attempt to frighten him.

'I'm not scared of little piggies!' he said.

'Well, you should be. They'll trotter you away.'

'Trotter me away!'

'Trotters, snouts, teeth! They use anything to get rid of you.'

'What they lack in size they make up for in cunning,' chipped in Mr Snuffle. 'But do as your poor mother says, Truffle – pick up your clothes – and you won't hear a squeal out of them.'

Unfortunately, Truffle now had the bit between his teeth. He was convinced that the Clothes Pigs were just a story that his parents had made up to correct his behaviour.

'I don't believe you,' he said boldly. 'I mean, for a start, I live in a city, and pigs are country animals. How are these Clothes Pigs going to get to me? Are they going to walk through the middle of a busy city in broad daylight? Do they know how to use a pelican crossing? Are they going to saunter past every Butchers Shop without being chased with a carving knife? I don't think so, do you?' This merely confirmed how pig-ignorant Truffle *was*. That is to say, how ignorant he was of the power of pigs!

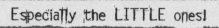
Especially the LITTLE ones!

＊ ＊ ＊

Then the accident happened and Truffle's life went apple-sauce shaped.

His mother was carrying a pile of his washing across the landing when she tripped on a pant-hill that he'd left at the top of the stairs. She didn't stand a chance. She fell forward, only to find that the ground had disappeared from underneath her, and flew through the air until the stairs broke her fall. Sadly, they also broke her leg. She bumped down the last three steps and crumpled into a heap on the hall floor.

'Aaaagh!' she wailed. 'I've broken my leg!' Truffle came running, but didn't seem to notice the pain that his mother was in.

'Where's my lunch?' he said. 'I'm hungry.'

'Help!' she cried. 'Call me an ambulance!'

'You're an ambulance. Now get up and cook!'

She tried. Give Mrs Snuffle her due, she tried to stand up and create something tasty and nutritious from cheese and toast, but her leg couldn't support her weight and she collapsed again. So Truffle took £5 out of her purse and went out for fish and chips instead.

'You're a hypocrite!' he said, turning in the doorway. 'What sort of example do you think you're setting me, lying there on the floor like that, in the middle of the day, like a great big lazy lump!'

'Don't leave me,' whispered his mother, but the front door had already been closed.

When Truffle came back, his mother was in traction and his father was in the garden, hanging out the washing. He was fuming.

'There you are,' he roared, his face flushing red. 'You and your piles of dropped clothes! How dare you leave your mother like that! She could have died.'

'I could have died of *hunger*, you mean,' Truffle replied cheekily, causing a reaction from his father the ferocity of which he had never seen before. It was an overheated-steam-engine-boiler of an explosion!

'YOU ARE A SELFISH LITTLE BOY, TRUFFLE!' he hollered. 'I WISH THE CLOTHES PIGS WOULD COME AND TEACH YOU A LESSON RIGHT NOW!'

His father's voice was so choked with fury that it came out as a high-pitched squeak. The resulting sound waves caused the air to vibrate so fast that the clothes line quivered. It sang like a mournful violin string and sent a spooky hum down the line. From one garden to the next, clothes lines trembled and passed on the sound of Mr Snuffle's voice, carrying his message into the countryside like a telephone cable.

When his voice arrived at Cherry Tree Farm, the four tiny piglets, Insy, Winsy, Nibble and Titch, were so hungry that they hadn't got out of bed for a week. They had started to wonder if they would ever eat again. So when they heard Mr Snuffle's despairing cry come down the wire they pricked up their ears and leaped to their feet.

'Problem in the Snuffle house!' cried Winsy. 'Call for the Clothes Pigs!' Insy and Titch cheered and sang a merry song . . .

> '*We're going to eat*
> *We're going to eat*
> *We're clothing up*
> *For boy meat!*'

. . . while Nibble rolled his eyes and sniffed the air. 'I smell Truffle!' he cried.

'And we do love truffles!' the brothers squealed as one.

The Clothes Pigs wasted no time in sorting out their affairs and setting off in a hurry for the big city, letting themselves out of the gate with a wave to Big Bertha and a collective grunt to their mother, informing her that they would be back soon.

'Whatever,' she replied. Unlike human beings, pigs are remarkably relaxed about letting their children get on with their lives.

On the way to the big city, Insy, Winsy, Nibble and Titch stopped in

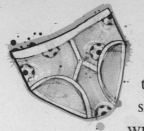

several gardens to pick up supplies. In the first garden they jumped into a peg trug sitting beside a washing line, wriggled down into the wooden pegs and waited until a woman appeared with a basket full of washing.

While she was choosing a shirt from the basket they lay ram-rod still, holding their front legs high above their heads as if frozen in the middle of a Mexican Wave, and their back legs stretched straight down like a ballerina on point. It fooled her. When the woman picked up a peg from the trug it was Nibble. He grabbed onto the washing line with his front trotters while she pushed the shoulder of the shirt into his rear trotters, picked up Insy and put the other shoulder into his.

Two minutes later, Winsy and Titch had joined their brothers on the line clutching in *their* trotters a splendid pair of brown corduroy trousers. When the woman went back indoors, they simply let go of the line, dropped to the ground and ran off with their booty.

And so it went on, from garden to garden. The four little piglets were picked up and pegged out on washing lines, until they had accumulated enough clothes to make one complete outfit.

And *this* was how they entered the big city without being seen: disguised as a human being, wearing brown trousers, a pink shirt, blue socks, a crew neck jumper, a thick woollen overcoat, a black Homburg hat, and sunglasses (which Titch had pinched off a table outside a pub). The Clothes Pigs made themselves the size and shape of a man by climbing onto each other's shoulders and forming a pig-pole. Nibble was the face – he wore the shades and had to do all of the talking. Titch drew the short straw and got the legs, while Insy and Winsy stood on his shoulders and provided an arm each. With every passing minute dinner came closer and closer. They walked through the town with a smile for every butcher and a wave for every passer-by . .
.

'Morning!'

'Morning!'

'Morning!' they cried, as they tipped their hat to the ladies. And nobody suspected a thing.

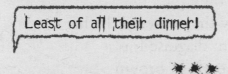

Least of all their dinner!

* * *

When the Clothes Pigs arrived at Truffle's house, Mrs Snuffle was resting and Mr Snuffle was weeding the front garden, so they were able to sneak in through the cat flap. On the mat inside the back door, they found a pile of Truffle's clothes lying exactly where he had dropped them a few hours earlier. Jumping down off each other's shoulders, they stripped off their stolen clothes, hid them in the coal hole in case a speedy exit was required, then slipped into Truffle's clothes. Just in time, as it happened.

'Who's there?' called out Truffle's mother from her sick bed. When there was no reply, Mr Snuffle came to investigate, but all he saw was a back view of Truffle sitting at the table hunched over a comic. He couldn't see his face or hair, because Truffle was wearing his hoodie, but it was definitely his son. Those were his clothes.

'Oh, it's you,' said Mr Snuffle. 'I thought I heard oinking.'

The Clothes Pigs had three hours to kill before Truffle came home. With nothing to do, their thoughts naturally turned to how hungry they all were.

'I'm famished,' squeaked Titch.

'I'm starving,' groaned Nibble.

'I'm *both*,' said Insy, who hadn't taken his eyes off the fridge for ninety-two minutes. 'Just a teeny-weeny snack,' he dribbled feebly. 'Please!'

'No,' said Winsy. 'You don't want to spoil your dinner.'

When dinner returned home from school at five o'clock, the Clothes Pigs snapped into action. It was vital that they were not spotted in the same room as Truffle lest Mr and Mrs Snuffle, seeing two sons, smelled a rat. If Truffle walked into a room, therefore, the Clothes Pigs shot out of the other door. Naturally there were mix-ups when the pigs accidentally ran into

Mrs Snuffles's bedroom and found themselves standing at the foot of her bed – but, luckily, her plastered leg (which was raised up in a harness) obscured her view. This meant that she never clocked Nibble's face.

She did, however, give them a scare when she asked suddenly, 'Why have you changed your clothes? When you rushed past my door a minute ago you were wearing something different.'

'Jam,' improvised Nibble. He had chosen the shortest word he could think of so that she had less time to realise that it wasn't her son's voice. 'Covered in jam!' Then he kicked Insy and Winsy's shoulders, which was the signal to scram, and they in turn kicked Titch's shoulders, who ran out of the room as fast as his little legs would carry them.

Watching Truffle eat his supper through a crack in the kitchen door was a painful experience. The pigs' stomachs gurgled and groaned as he ate his sausages.

'I wish he'd hurry up,' wept Insy.

'Patience,' said Nibble. 'Not long now.'

Finally, just before bedtime, the Clothes Pigs sneaked into Truffle's bedroom and hid under his bed, where they waited patiently for their dinner to be served. And waited.

And waited. And waited.

And waited.

'There's an awful lot of waiting being a Clothes Pig,' whispered Insy.

'But it's worth it in the end,' said Nibble, 'Ssssh!'

The shadow of the boy had just entered the room. Behind him, Truffle had left a trail of discarded clothes up the stairs. By the time he reached the edge of the bed, four pairs of piggy eyes had fixed him firmly in their sights. Their tummies rumbled as they gazed longingly upon their first food in a fortnight. He switched off his bedside light and climbed into bed. The springs creaked over the pigs' heads. They waited some more until Truffle had stopped fidgeting and started to snore. Finally, he was asleep.

'Ready?' whispered Titch, wiping his wet lips with the back of his trotter. 'Then let the eating begin!'

And the Clothes Pigs emerged from under the bed to a feast!

In case you weren't paying attention earlier, pigs aren't fussy what they eat. Bone, gristle, ears, eyes, teeth, hair, toenails, they'll eat anything, right down to the buttons on a boy's pyjamas!

In the morning, the Clothes Pigs had gone . . . just like Truffle, in fact. They left the clothes they had borrowed in a heap by the side of his bed, and on the way home they revisited those gardens whence they had stolen their man-clothes, and hung · them back up on the washing lines. Clothes Pigs may be many things, but they are not thieves. Then they returned to Cherry Tree Farm for a long sleep in the sunshine and to wait for their next invitation to dinner!

Your choice is simple; PICK UP or PIG! If you can't decide which one is for you just remember that picking up clothes can be very painful on the back, whereas being eaten by a pig is not painful at all. It's just a question of filling your head with pretty thoughts to take your mind off the pigs' teeth hacking hunks off you.

'HEEEEEEEEEEEEEEEELP!'

Oh, this is too much. I know I shouldn't, but he does go on!

That should shut him up permanently.

Now, where were we? Oh yes, now that you've decided to stay we need to fill out a Registration Form.

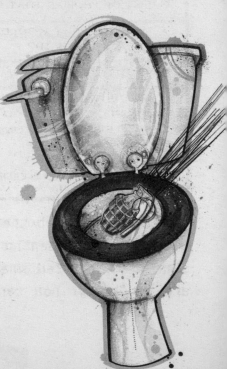